Sophie Skates

Rachel Isadora

PUFFIN BOOKS

For my father
with whom I share
a love of ice skating

PUFFIN BOOKS
Published by the Penguin Group
Penguin Putnam Books for Young Readers, 345 Hudson Street, New York, New York 10014, U.S.A.
Penguin Books Ltd, 27 Wrights Lane, London W8 5TZ, England
Penguin Books Australia Ltd, Ringwood, Victoria, Australia
Penguin Books Canada Ltd, 10 Alcorn Avenue, Toronto, Ontario, Canada M4V 3B2
Penguin Books (N.Z.) Ltd, 182-190 Wairau Road, Auckland 10, New Zealand
Penguin Books Ltd, Registered Offices: Harmondsworth, Middlesex, England

First published in the United States of America by G.P. Putnam's Sons, a division of Penguin Putnam Books for Young Readers, 1999
Published by Puffin Books, a division of Penguin Putnam Books for Young Readers, 2001

10 9 8 7 6 5 4 3 2 1

Copyright © Rachel Isadora, 1999. All rights reserved.

THE LIBRARY OF CONGRESS HAS CATALOGED THE G. P. PUTNAM'S SONS EDITION AS FOLLOWS:
Isadora, Rachel. Sophie skates / Rachel Isadora. p. cm.
Summary: Uses a story about a young girl who loves to ice skate to introduce the sport: the parts and care of the skates, the techniques of different skating moves, and ice skating competitions. [1. Skating—Juvenile literature. 2. Ice skating.] I. Title.
GV850.4.I73 1999 [796.91 21]—dc21 98-21930 CIP AC ISBN 0-399-23046-7

Puffin Books ISBN 0-698-11905-3   Printed in the United States of America

Except in the United States of America, this book is sold subject to the condition that it shall not, by way of trade or otherwise, be lent, re-sold, hired out, or otherwise circulated without the publisher's prior consent in any form of binding or cover other than that in which it is published and without a similar condition including this condition being imposed on the subsequent purchaser.

Sophie started skating when she was three years old,
on the pond behind her house.

Now Sophie is eight years old. She dreams of becoming a professional ice skater, but she knows there will be many years of hard work ahead.

Sophie watches ice skating on television, but most of all she likes going to ice skating shows. There she gets to see the skating up close. She claps hard for the performers and can't wait for the day when the applause is for her.

Sophie takes lessons five mornings and three afternoons a week. Her morning class begins at five o'clock! When she arrives, some of her friends are already warming up. She says hello to Mr. Simon, the coach.

short leg warmers

thin socks

pants with stirrups

Eddie has
taken off his
warm-up suit.

warm-up suit

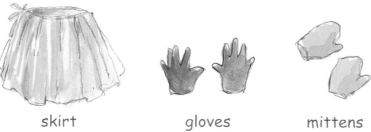

skirt

gloves

mittens

Everyone is dressed warmly. The ice rink
can be very cold, so the skaters wear layers
of clothing that they take off as they warm
up. Skaters choose clothes that are easy to
move in but still fit close to the body.

leotard

leotard with skirt

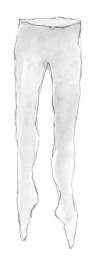

tights

sweater

long leg warmers

Charlie's mother really bundled him up!

Sophie's skates are already broken in. When they were new, they felt stiff and hurt her feet. She had to put guards over the blades and walk around her house to soften the leather.

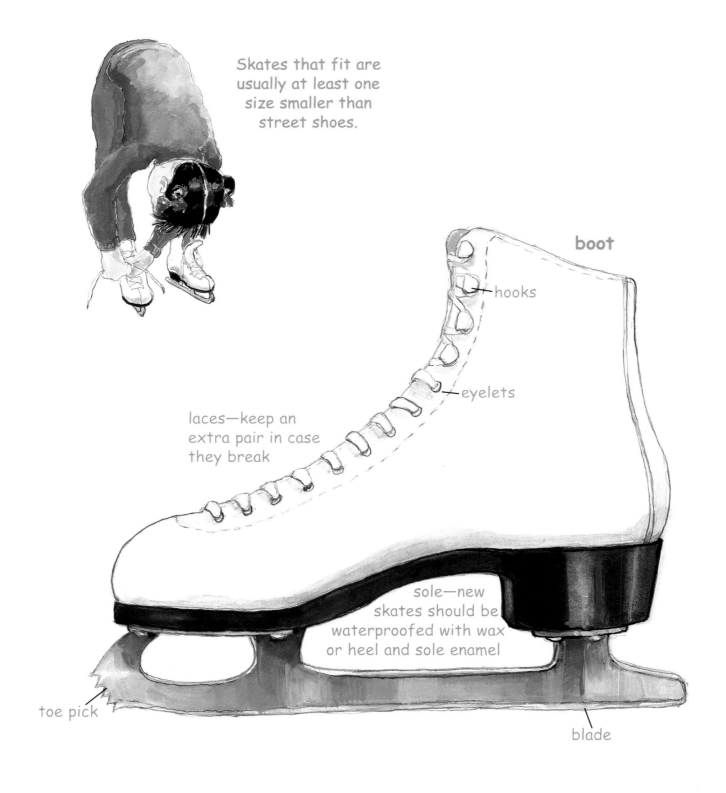

Skates that fit are usually at least one size smaller than street shoes.

boot

hooks

eyelets

laces—keep an extra pair in case they break

sole—new skates should be waterproofed with wax or heel and sole enamel

toe pick

blade

Always use blade
guards when you
wear skates off
the ice.

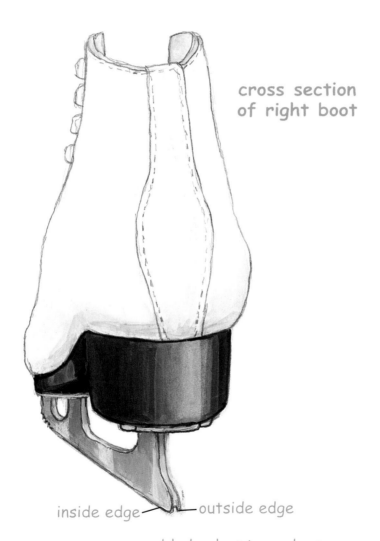

**cross section
of right boot**

inside edge———outside edge

blade—has two edges,
inside and outside,
because the bottom
is concave

Sophie can lace up her skates quickly. But when she was first learning, it took a long time to do it correctly.

Make sure you pull the laces tightly as you go, especially around the ankle. A snug fit gives support. When new skates are laced correctly, there should be two inches of space between the two lines of eyelets. As skates get broken in, the leather stretches and the lacing gets closer.

Max tied his skates too loosely, so he doesn't have ankle support.

Pamela forgot to tuck in her
laces. Tuck the loops and
ends between the laces
and the tongue. Lace loops
should never dangle!

Maggie is ready
to go! Perfect!

Mr. Simon begins the morning class with the basics. Young skaters do these skills over and over again. Learning to get up from a fall gracefully is always important.

Mohawk

"Twist your hips quickly just as you turn."

"Don't get your leg too high."

fishies

"Look where you are going, not down."

"Don't let your knees or toes touch."

fishies pattern— forward and backward

backward wiggles

"Move your hips from side to side and pretend you're a puppy wagging your tail."

three turn

Basics include different ways to stop as well as different ways to move. Some basics are practiced both forward and backward, or with just the right foot and just the left foot.

"Remember to hold up your back, and don't bend at the hips or waist."

"Keep your thighs close together."

This turn is called a "three" because the pattern your skates make on the ice looks like the number three.

getting up from the ice

"The blade has to be flat on the ice."

"Remember to get up by balancing with your arms."

After basics, Sophie's class practices figures. Figures are difficult, but they help the students learn to glide with control. Everyone takes turns skating on the ice, using all four edges.

Then they do basic eights, which are skated in two circles that make the shape of an eight. "It's good we skate eights, and not fours," Pamela says and they all laugh, even Mr. Simon. At seven A.M., class is over and everyone leaves for school.

The four basic types of figure eights use the four edges: forward inside, forward outside, back outside, and back inside.

After school, Sophie returns to the rink for a private lesson in free skating. She does her jumps, spins, and footwork over and over again.

one foot spin

standard spin preparation

entry

spin

forward spiral

As her muscles get stronger, she will jump higher, spin faster, and move with more control.

toe loop

take off   in the air   landing

layback spin

Sophie wants every move to be perfect. But she's been skating long enough to know that sometimes she will fall. When it happens, she tries not to be hard on herself.

lunge

ooops

sit spin

camel spin

Sophie takes ballet lessons two after-noons a week. Some of her friends from ice skating class are in her ballet class, too!

split

développé

extension

jump

Ballet helps them be more flexible and graceful on the ice.

á la seconde
stretch

port de bras
stretch

butterfly

shoot the duck

Competing is Sophie's favorite part of ice skating. A big competition is coming up in three weeks. In her afternoon class, Sophie runs through her short program with Ms. Wilkin, the choreographer.

The short program, also called the technical program, is two minutes, forty seconds long. There are eight required elements which can be done in any sequence. The short program counts for one-third of a skater's score.

She tries on her costumes and decides on the purple one.
"This brought me good luck last competition," she says, and
does a super jump.

The long program, also called free skate, is four minutes for women, four and a half minutes for men. There are no required elements. Skaters choreograph their program to showcase their best technical and artistic skills. The long program counts for two-thirds of a skater's score.

Sophie is excited to skate her long program. She agrees with Ms. Wilkin on the bright green costume. It matches the happy music. "I won't have to remember to smile," Sophie says. "This program is so much fun!"

It is time to go home. Before they leave the stadium, Sophie and her mom stop and watch Nick lift his partner high in the air. Sophie applauds. Suddenly Nick skates over and scoops up Sophie and lifts her high in the air, too. "I'm flying!" she shouts.

After dinner, Sophie cleans and dries her skates. She sits with her dog, Henry, and does her homework. It's nice to be home after a long day.

"Get your skates, Sophie! Let's go out to the pond!" her brother calls a little later.

But Sophie is already asleep.